To Betsy
—D. C.

To John William Reilly.
Welcome to the world.
—B. L.

Atheneum Books for Young Readers · An imprint of Simon & Schuster Children's Publishing Division · 1230 Avenue of the Americas · New York, New York 10020 · Text copyright © 2008 by Doreen Cronin · Illustrations copyright © 2008 by Betsy Lewin · All rights reserved, including the right of reproduction in whole or in part in any form. · Book design by Ann Bobco · The text for this book is set in Filosofia. · The illustrations for this book are rendered in brush and watercolor. · Manufactured in the United States of America · First Edition · 10 9 8 7 6 5 4 3 2 1 · Library of Congress Cataloging-in-Publication Data · Cronin, Doreen. · Thump, quack, moo : a whacky adventure / Doreen Cronin ; illustrated by Betsy Lewin. — 1st ed. · p. cm. · Summary: The annual Corn Maze Festival is coming, and every day the chickens, cows, and Duck help Farmer Brown— with a few bribes—to create a special Statue of Liberty corn maze, and every night Duck works hard recreating his own surprise. · ISBN-13: 978-1-4169-1630-7 · ISBN-10: 1-4169-1630-X · [1. Ducks—Fiction. 2. Domestic animals—Fiction. 3. Farmers—Fiction. 4. Festivals—Fiction.] I. Lewin, Betsy, ill. II. Title. · PZ7.C88135Th 2008 · [E]—dc22 · 2007044075

Thump, Quack, Moo

A Whacky Adventure

by **Doreen Cronin**
and **Betsy Lewin**

Atheneum Books for Young Readers · New York London Toronto Sydney

It is almost time for the annual Corn Maze Festival.

Farmer Brown is very excited.

This year he is making a Statue of Liberty corn maze.

He is going to need help to get everything ready on time.

The chickens do not want to help.
"I'll let you use my hammers,"
said Farmer Brown.

The chickens are now building the fence around the corn field.

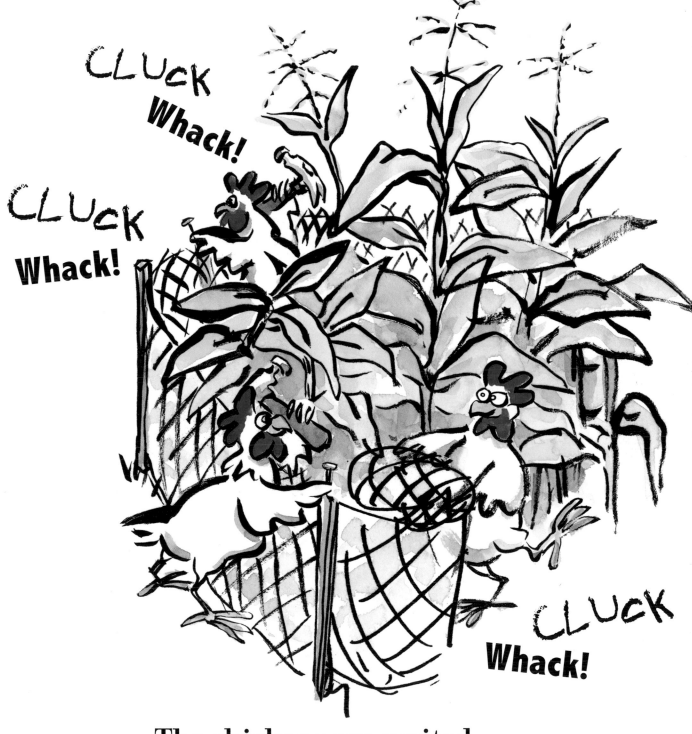

The chickens are excited.

The cows do not want to help.
"I'll let you use my paintbrushes,"
said Farmer Brown.

The cows are now giving the barn
a fresh coat of paint.

The cows are excited.

Duck never wants to help.
"No help," said Farmer Brown to Duck,
"no more special-order organic duck feed."

Thump

Quack.

Thump

Quack.

Duck is still not excited.

The mice are taking a correspondence course on meteorology and are too busy to lend a hand.

PARTLY SUNNY

HUMIDITY 60%

The air is filled
with the busy sounds
of the farm.

Thump. QUACK!

The mice keep an eye on the weather.

INCREASING CLOUDS

WIND ADVISORY IN EFFECT

Farmer Brown is busy too.
Every day he gets out his
sketch book, graph paper,
art supplies, and mower.

He sketches a little . . .

measures a little . . .

counts a little . . .

. . . and cuts. Farmer Brown wants it perfect.

Every night Duck sneaks into the corn field.
He brings his sketch book, graph paper,
art supplies, and hedge clippers.
He also brings his night-vision goggles
and glow-in-the-dark ruler.
Then he sketches a little . . .

measures a little . . .

counts a little . . .

The mice keep an eye on the weather.

It is the day before the annual Corn Maze Festival.
For the last time Farmer Brown gets out his
sketch book, graph paper, art supplies, and mower.

He sketches a little . . .
measures a little . . .
counts a little . . .
and cuts.

The Statue of Liberty corn maze is finished!
He is too excited to sleep.

Duck sneaks into the corn field for the last time. He brings his sketch book, graph paper, art supplies, and hedge clippers. He also brings his night-vision goggles and glow-in-the-dark ruler.

Then he sketches a little . . .
measures a little . . .
counts a little . . .
and cuts.

He is too excited to sleep.

It is time for the Corn Maze Festival opening ceremony!

The chickens are not allowed to use the hammers anymore.

The barn is not quite what Farmer Brown had in mind.

The ticket booth has
a slight design flaw.

But all Farmer Brown cares about is the corn maze.

He pays five dollars and hops into the hot-air balloon.

At last he will see his masterpiece from above!

Duck also pays five dollars and hops into the hot-air balloon.

At last he will see his masterpiece from above!

Duck is really excited now!

GERONIMO!